To everyone who has ever climbed a tree . . .
or wanted to. —J.D.

For my sons, Otto & Felix. —R.G.

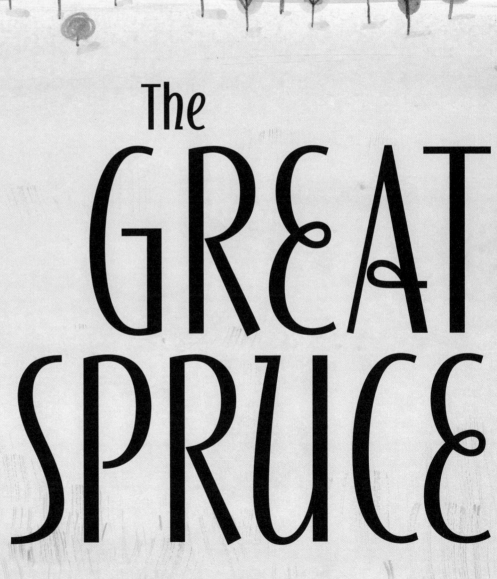

The
GREAT
SPRUCE

John Duvall illustrated by Rebecca Gibbon

G. P. PUTNAM'S SONS

ALEC LOVED TO CLIMB TREES.

He climbed all the trees in town: the little apple trees,
the wide willow trees, even the tall locust trees.

But the tree he liked to climb the most was the
great spruce. It was the most magical of all the trees,
tall and strong and spreading ever upward.

His grandpa told him many times the story of the year he transplanted the tree, a long time before Alec was born.

Digging carefully, he moved the little spruce from the shade of the forest floor to a sunny spot where the tree could stretch its arms and reach for the sky.

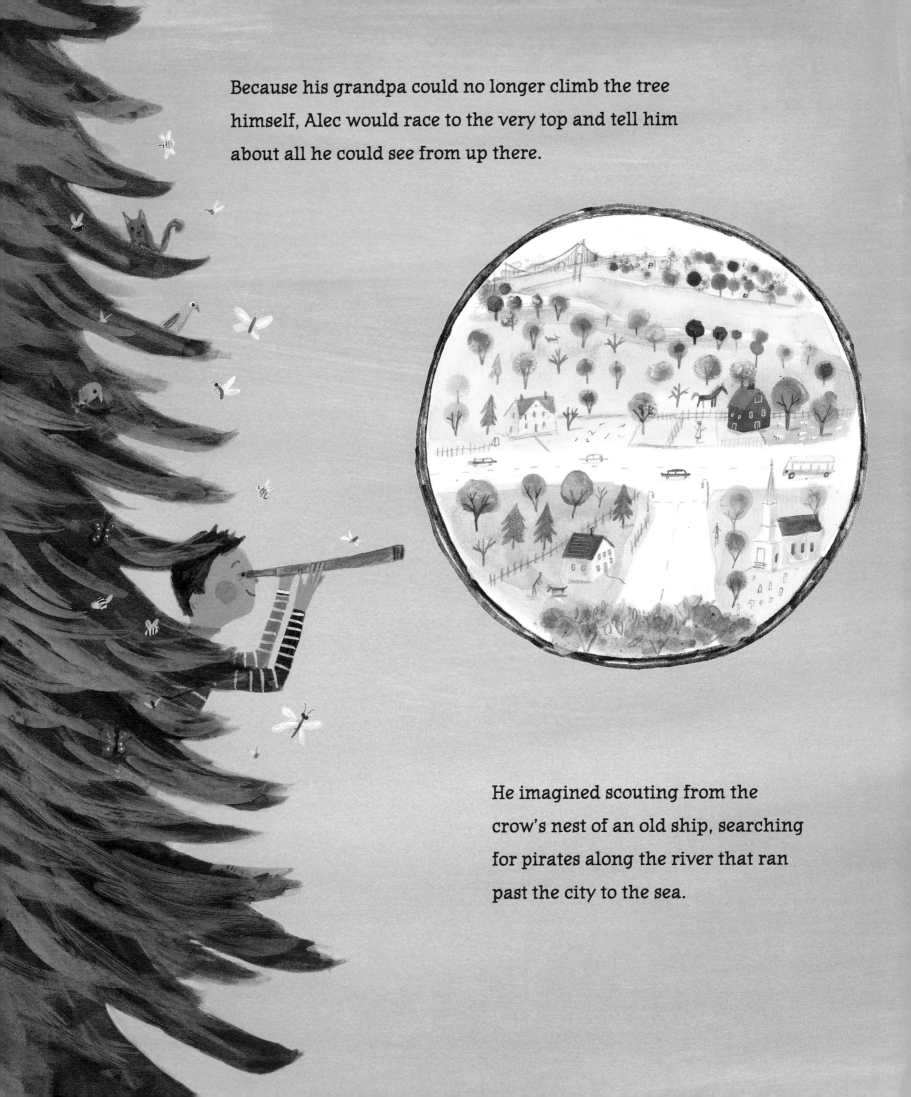

Because his grandpa could no longer climb the tree himself, Alec would race to the very top and tell him about all he could see from up there.

He imagined scouting from the crow's nest of an old ship, searching for pirates along the river that ran past the city to the sea.

EACH WINTER, Alec and his grandpa would decorate the tree.

"Our tree likes lots of lights and tinsel," Grandpa told Alec.

When they were done, their tree shone like a Christmas tree lighthouse.

ONE DAY, Alec was collecting spruce cones in the upper branches when a few curious men stopped to look at the tree.

One of the men knocked on Alec's front door.

When Alec's parents appeared, the men asked if they could take
the great spruce for the Christmas celebration in the city.
Alec's parents thought it would be a great honor and agreed.
But Alec could not believe what he heard. His tree would be gone forever!

Days later, a crew arrived to remove the tree with a giant chain saw.

Everyone in town came to watch.

The saw started up and it was terribly loud. But Alec was even louder when he screamed, "STOP!"

The tall man turned off the saw. A breeze blew through the branches of the great spruce, whispering a sigh of relief.

"You don't have to cut this tree down," Alec said. He was shaking and felt so many eyes on him, but when he found his grandpa's face in the crowd, he knew. "We can dig it up! You can *borrow* the tree instead!"

Alec's grandpa, with a
smile as bright as any star,
grabbed two shovels and
handed one to Alec.

Before long, everyone was digging,
even the crew from the city!

They began to dig a circle
around the tree.

When they finished digging, they wrapped the tree's
huge root ball with burlap and big, thick rope.

The city sent a tugboat with a mighty crane to lift the tree from the earth and hoist it onto the boat.

The crew asked Alec if he'd like to join them on the voyage down the river to the city. "Can my grandpa come, too?" Alec asked.

AND SO THEY SET OFF down the dark and beautiful river as the townspeople and his parents cheered from the dock. Alec held his grandpa's hand as they sat, bundled up and excited, alongside the great spruce.

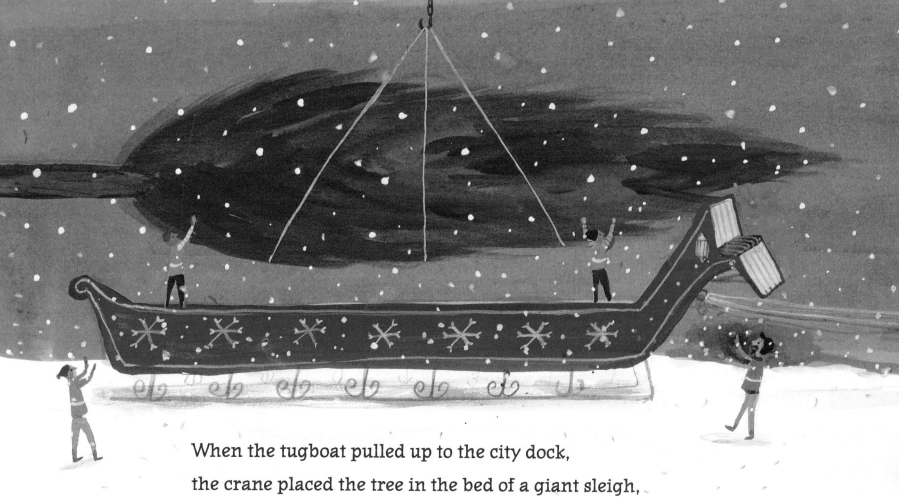

When the tugboat pulled up to the city dock,

the crane placed the tree in the bed of a giant sleigh,

which was waiting with a team of horses to take
the great spruce on the last leg of its journey.

UP CLOSE, the city smelled like smoke, and wind blew through the tall buildings.

Car horns honked, a woman laughed, and Alec, his grandpa,
and the great spruce moved slowly through the streets
among cheers and songs from happy faces.

They arrived at the city square, and a team of men and women helped move the great spruce into a special place at the center of the square.

Alec and his grandpa drank hot chocolate
and waited as the officials, his parents, and
face after familiar face from home arrived
at the square, gathering around the
great spruce.

FINALLY, an official, tall and dressed in a fancy suit, announced to all gathered, "This is our young friend Alec, who is lending us his tree for the holiday. Please help me thank him as he throws the switch!"

The crowd cried out in joy at the sight of the
magnificent spruce and its many colored lights.
It smelled like Christmas, and a hush fell over
the city for just a minute.

Suddenly, a young girl atop her father's shoulders
shouted, "It's the most wonderful tree in the world!
Can it stay here forever?"

"We're just visiting," said Alec. "But here,
take this cone. It has seeds inside.
Plant them in good soil, with lots of
light, and don't forget to water them!"

AFTER THE HOLIDAYS, the great spruce returned home to the earth. Alec gave it plenty of water, and by the spring, the big tree had grown even taller.

Alec could see a bit farther down the river, and if he looked hard enough through his telescope, he could just make out the tiny sapling that took root in the big city square.

AUTHOR'S NOTE

Have you ever wondered where the Christmas tree tradition comes from?
It is said that a preacher started the tradition a very long time ago in the 1500s.
He was walking home one winter night when he saw stars twinkling between
the evergreens. It was such a beautiful sight, he went right home to re-create the
scene for his family. He put a tree in the main room and fastened its branches
with lighted candles. His family agreed it was beautiful.

In an effort to bring some of that same beauty and cheer during the Great Depression,
construction workers placed a freshly cut twenty-foot balsam tree in New York City's
Rockefeller Center, decorating it with tin cans and garlands. The tradition continued
annually, until almost ten years later, when the center decided for the first time
to bring in three living trees—the tallest measured fifty feet. After the holiday,
the live spruce trees were replanted on the Long Island estates where they came from.
And for the next few years, the center continued to celebrate with living trees.

But then the tradition changed again. Likely because it costs more money and
takes more work to dig and move a tree than it does to cut one down, the center
returned to installing cut trees. But just imagine if that very first tree used to
celebrate Christmas at Rockefeller Center in 1931 had been dug and replanted.
It might still be alive today!

For a long time now, I've been moving live trees and watching them grow beautifully
for years. I work to keep trees alive every chance I get. There is no need to cut down
a tree for people to enjoy it. If a tree can live to be hundreds of years old, then why not
let it? After all, trees give life to other trees around them, their leaves and needles
fall each year and provide essential food for the earth, and they are a habitat for
birds, bugs, and many of our other friends in the forest. And don't forget one of a
tree's other important jobs: They provide a place for kids to climb high and look out
over the world, perhaps seeing things no one else can.

TRANSPLANTING A TREE

PHOTO 1: After the lower branches are carefully tied up to provide room to dig, the digging operation begins. PHOTO 2: Very sharp shovels, picks, and pruning shears are used to care for the roots as they dig. PHOTO 3: When the digging is done, burlap and twine are set out to wrap the root ball. PHOTO 4: The root ball is tied in a drum lace pattern to secure the soil and roots. PHOTO 5: All secure, the tree is ready to move.

G. P. PUTNAM'S SONS
an imprint of Penguin Random House LLC
375 Hudson Street, New York, NY 10014

Text copyright © 2016 by John Duvall. Illustrations copyright © 2016 by Rebecca Gibbon.

Library of Congress Cataloging-in-Publication Data is available upon request.

Manufactured in China by RR Donnelley Asia Printing Solutions Ltd. / ISBN 978-0-399-16084-4 / 10 9 8 7 6 5 4 3 2 1

Design by Ryan Thomann. Text set in Journal. The art was done in acrylic ink and colored pencil on acid-free Cartridge paper.